Classic Tales
Level 4

T0308247

The Goose Girl

Retold by Sue Arengo
Illustrated by Elena Selivanova

Contents

OXFORD
UNIVERSITY PRESS

Once upon a time there was a queen who had only one beautiful daughter. She loved the girl very much.

At last, the day came for the princess to go far away and marry a prince. The queen was sad to say goodbye.

She gave her daughter some beautiful dresses, a gold cup, and many other things. She gave her a magic horse. It was a white horse and it could talk.

'I love this horse, Mother,' the princess said. 'I will call it Falada!'

And the queen gave her daughter a maid to ride with her.

Then the queen made three drops of blood fall onto a handkerchief.

'Take this,' she said to her daughter. 'It will help you. It will make you strong. Now goodbye, daughter. And be happy!'

The princess took the handkerchief with the three drops of blood. She put it inside her dress.

'Goodbye, Mother!' she said. 'Thank you for everything!'

The queen watched them ride away down the long hill.

It was a very hot day. Soon the princess was thirsty. They were near a stream and so she asked her maid, 'Maid! Please will you get me a drink of water in my gold cup?'

But the maid said angrily, 'No! I will not! You get off your horse and get it! I will not be your maid!'

The princess did not know what to say. So she got off her horse and went to the stream and drank.

Then they rode on. But the sun was warm and later she asked again, 'Maid! Please will you get me a drink of water in my gold cup?'

And again the maid said angrily, 'No! I will not! You get off your horse and get it! I will not be your maid!'

The princess did not know what to say. So she got off her horse and went to the stream and drank. But this time the handkerchief fell into the water.

'Ah! That's good!' thought the maid. 'There is no one here. And now she has nothing to help her.'

So she said to the princess, 'Take off that dress and give it to me! You can wear my grey one. Be quick now or I will kill you! And I will have Falada. I am going to be the princess. I am going to be the bride. And you are going to be my maid!'

So they rode on. The maid rode in front on Falada. The princess rode behind her on the old grey horse.

In the evening they arrived at the castle. The king and his son, the prince, came to meet them.

'How do you do, Princess?' said the king to the maid. 'This is my son, the prince!'

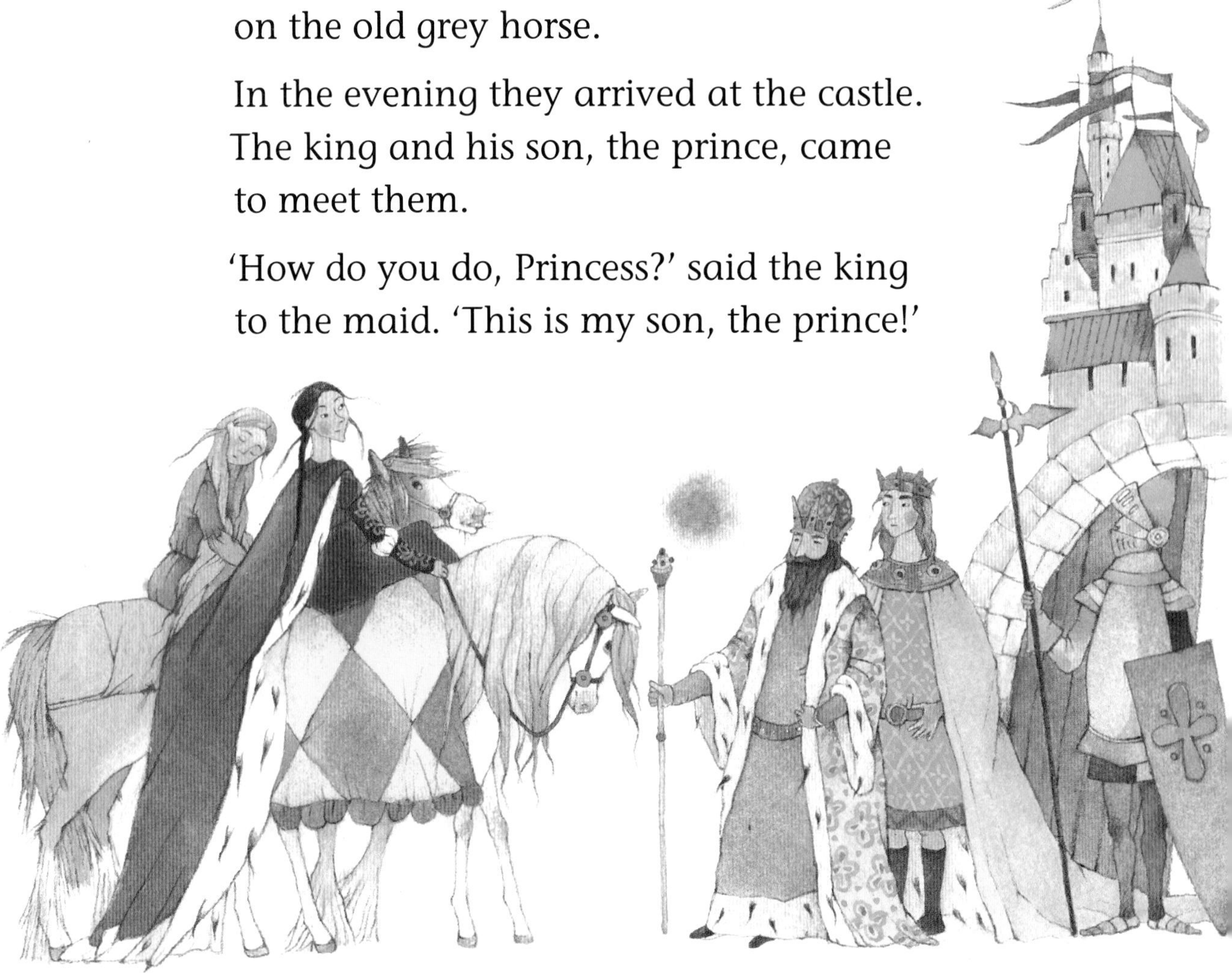

The real princess was left outside, but the king saw her.

'Who is that girl?' he thought. 'She has a beautiful face!'

‘Who are you?’ asked the king.

‘I came here as a maid,’ the real princess answered, ‘but you have many maids and you do not need me.’

‘I can find some work for you. You can be a goose girl,’ said the king. ‘Come with me.’

He took her to a little house near the castle gate.

‘This is Kirsten’s house,’ he said. ‘She looks after the geese! Kirsten! Come! Here’s a nice girl to help you! Give her some food and a bed, please.’

That night there was a big dinner at the castle.

'This princess is going to be my son's bride,' said the king. 'They will marry in three weeks.'

The maid looked at all the people and smiled.

Later that night she spoke to the prince.

'I have something to tell you,' she said. 'That white horse, Falada, is a bad horse. It's mad! You must kill it!'

She was afraid because Falada could talk.

'Yes, my bride,' said the prince, 'if you want that. I will tell my men to take it away.'

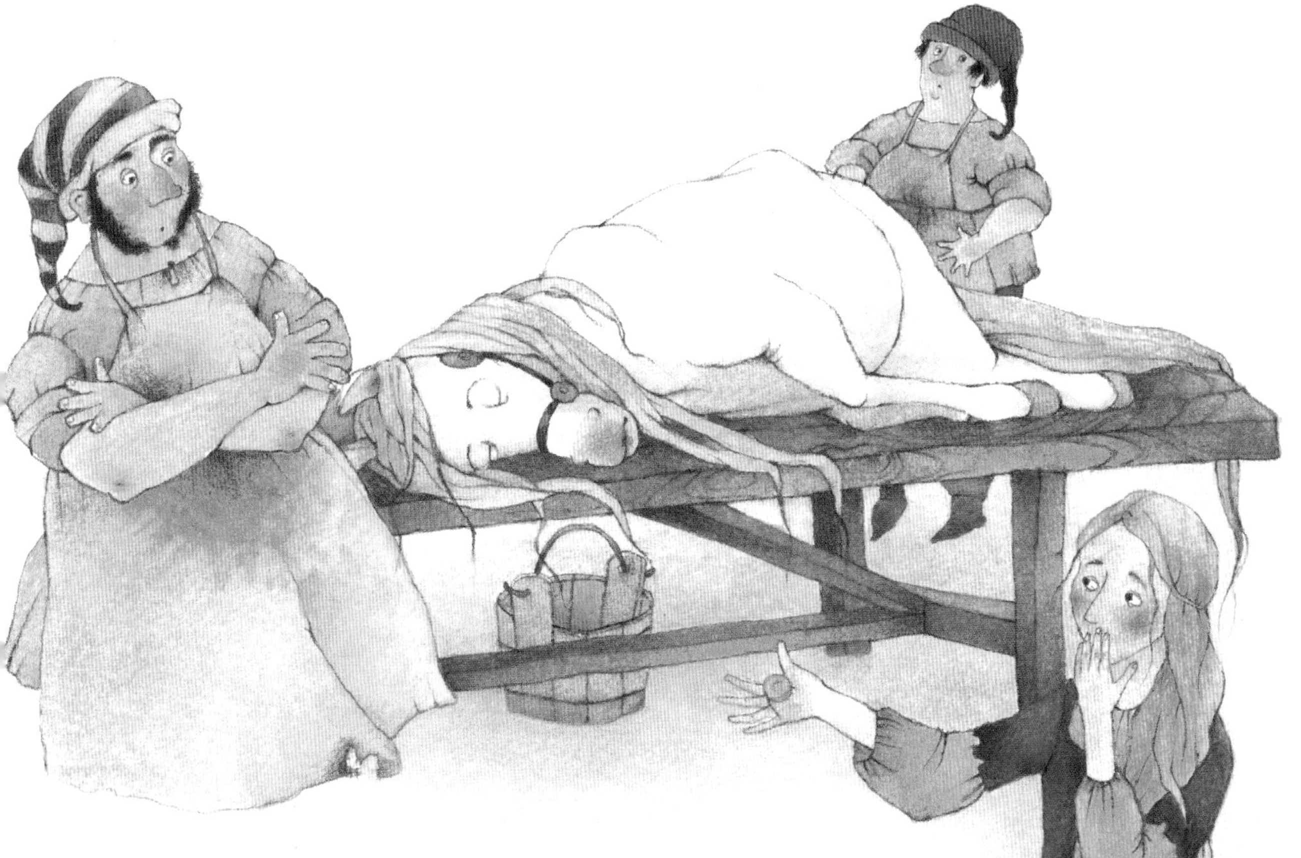

The real princess heard about this. She had one gold coin. She ran to the men and said, 'Take this gold coin. Do something for me. Do you see this dead horse? Put this horse's head by the big castle gate.'

'What?' they said. 'That's a mad idea! Why?'

'Because I loved that horse,' she said. 'I want to see its face.'

The men liked her. So they took the gold coin. And they put Falada's head by the castle gate.

Every day Kirsten took the geese out to the meadow, and the real princess went with her. They walked through the castle gate. And every day the real princess spoke to Falada's head.

'Falada! My horse ... do you know me?'

'Yes, Princess!' the head answered. 'You are the true bride!'

Kirsten did not like it. She thought it was very strange.

Every day the real princess brushed her long gold hair. And Kirsten always said, 'Give me some of your hair! Oh, come on! Cut some off and give it to me!'

And the real princess always said, 'No, Kirsten! Stop it!'

But Kirsten wouldn't stop it. So the real princess had to sing to the wind.

'Blow, wind. Blow!' she sang.
'Blow Kirsten's hat, blow it
over there, so I have time
to brush my hair!'

Then a wind came and blew Kirsten's hat off.

Kirsten had to run all over the meadow. Then the real princess had time to brush her hair. All this made Kirsten angry.

'You're strange!' she said to the princess. 'Who are you? You talk to the wind! You talk to a dead horse's head! You're mad. You're a mad girl. I'm going to tell the king about you.'

So Kirsten went to the king and said, 'Listen! That girl is mad. I don't want to work with her again. Every day she talks to a dead horse's head. And it talks back to her. And she sings to the wind. She asks the wind to blow my hat off. I have to run all over the meadow!'

'Mmm!' said the king. 'I want to come and see this.'

So the next day the king hid and watched. And he saw that it was true.

The king heard the real princess speak to Falada's head.

'Falada! My horse! Do you know me?'

'Yes, Princess! You are the true bride.'

And in the meadow the king heard her sing to the wind.

'Blow, wind. Blow!' she sang. 'Blow Kirsten's hat, blow it over there, so I have time to brush my hair!'

He saw Kirsten's hat blow off. And he saw her run all over the meadow.

That evening the king said, 'Who are you? I watched you today. I saw some very strange things. What is your story?'

'Oh!' answered the princess, 'I cannot tell you my story. She will kill me if I tell you anything.'

The king thought. Then he said, 'I see – you are too afraid to tell me. You can't tell me. All right. I will go out of the room. And you can tell your story to this old cupboard.'

The princess needed to speak. So she got inside the old cupboard. It was dark, but it was warm. And in the dark, she told her story.

The king listened through a hole in the wall. He heard all she said.

'I am the real princess – the true bride. My maid is going to marry the prince. She took my dress. She took my horse, Falada. She rode it here. She made me ride behind her. I have no one to help me. She will kill me if I tell anyone.'

Then the king said, 'Do not be afraid! Come with me. It is time to make everything right.'

The king found the prince and all the people in the castle.

'Now,' he said. 'Listen carefully and do not say a word.'

Then he told them about the real princess. And they were happy. They could see that she was beautiful and good.

That night the true bride sat next to the prince. Her maid sat on his other side and did not know her.

After dinner, the king spoke to everybody.

'Listen!' said the king. 'I have a story to tell you all.

'Once there was a princess who had a maid. That princess had to ride far away to marry a prince. And the maid went with her. But on the way the maid said, "Give me your dress! And give me your horse! Or I will kill you! I am going to be the princess now – and I am going to marry the prince!"'

Then the king went up to the maid and said, 'Tell me what you think about this.'

And she answered, 'That's really bad! Put that bad maid on a horse – a mad, bad horse. And let the mad, bad horse throw her into the sea!'

'Right,' said the king, 'then this is what will happen to you!'

So the maid had to ride a mad, bad horse. And it threw her into the sea.

Then the prince married the real princess – the true bride. And they were very happy.

Exercises

1 Who is speaking? Write the name for 1–5. For number 6, what does the king say? Write one sentence.

1 'Take this. It will help you.' *the queen*

2 'That white horse, Falada, is a bad horse.' ______

3 'Falada! My horse ... do you know me?' ______

4 'Yes, Princess! You are the true bride!' ______

5 'Give me some of your hair!' ______

6 ______________________________ *the king*

2 Write the words.

behind off into at outside through next to ~~inside~~

1 The princess put the handkerchief *inside* her dress.

2 The maid made the princess ride ______ her.

3 They arrived at the castle but the real princess was left ______ .

4 That night there was a big dinner ______ the castle.

5 Every day Kirsten and the real princess walked ______ the castle gate to the meadow.

6 A wind came and blew Kirsten's hat ______ .

7 After the real princess told her story, she sat ______ the prince at dinner.

8 A mad, bad horse threw the maid ______ the sea.

3 Write the words and write the numbers.

magic real beautiful long ~~gold~~ hot

[3] a *gold* cup
[ ] a __________ horse
[ ] a __________ hill
[ ] __________ dresses
[ ] the __________ princess
[ ] a __________ day

4 Find the page and answer the questions.

1 What did the queen put on the handkerchief?

page 3 *Three drops of blood.*

2 What happened to the handkerchief at the stream?

________ ____________________

3 Where did the prince's men put Falada's head?

________ ____________________

4 Why did the real princess ask the wind to blow Kirsten's hat off?

________ ____________________

5 Where did the real princess go to tell her story?

________ ____________________

6 How did the king hear it?

________ ____________________

Glossary

blood

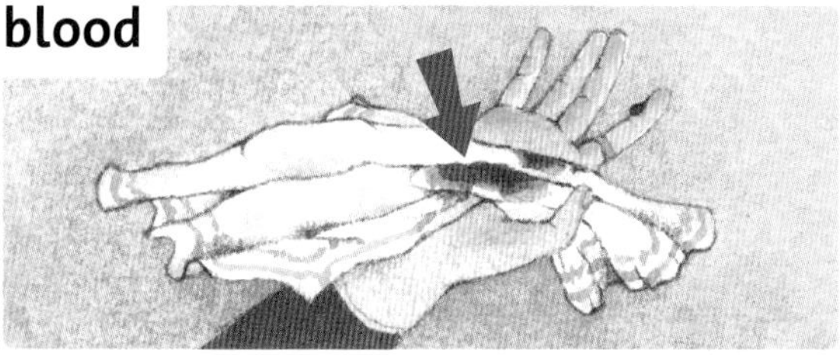

blow

bride a woman when she marries

brushed past tense of **brush**

castle

coin

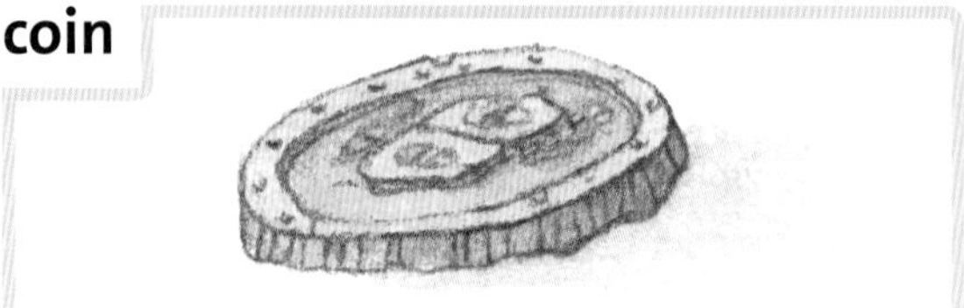

cupboard

drop a very small bit of liquid, eg water or blood

far away *She is far away.*

gate

gold *a gold cup*

goose

geese

handkerchief

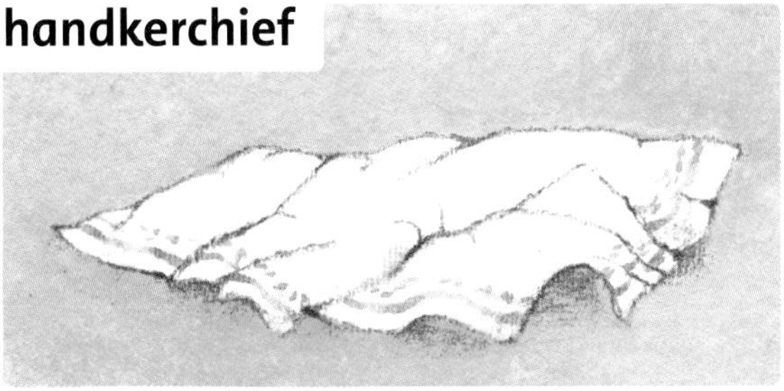

hid past tense of **hide**: to go where no one can see you

hole

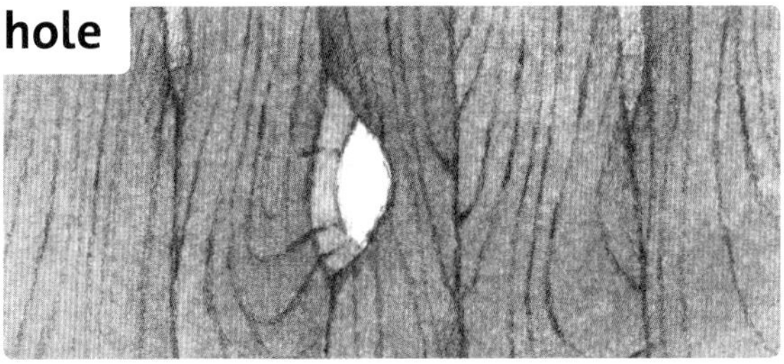

idea something you think of or decide to do

kill to make someone / something die

mad thinking and doing strange things

magic when things that seem impossible happen

maid a woman / girl who works for someone in their home

marry to become someone's husband / wife

meadow

real someone / something that is what they are called

ride

side *He's on the other side.*

stream a small river

true when something really happens

Classic Tales

Classic stories retold for learners of English – bringing the magic of traditional storytelling to the language classroom

Level 1: 100 headwords

- The Enormous Turnip
- The Little Red Hen
- Lownu Mends the Sky
- The Magic Cooking Pot
- Mansour and the Donkey
- Peach Boy
- The Princess and the Pea
- Rumpelstiltskin
- The Shoemaker and the Elves
- Three Billy-Goats

Level 2: 150 headwords

- Amrita and the Trees
- Big Baby Finn
- The Fisherman and his Wife
- The Gingerbread Man
- Jack and the Beanstalk
- Thumbelina
- The Town Mouse and the Country Mouse
- The Ugly Duckling

Level 3: 200 headwords

- Aladdin
- Goldilocks and the Three Bears
- The Little Mermaid
- Little Red Riding Hood

Level 4: 300 headwords

- Cinderella
- The Goose Girl
- Sleeping Beauty
- The Twelve Dancing Princesses

Level 5: 400 headwords

- Beauty and the Beast
- The Magic Brocade
- Pinocchio
- Snow White and the Seven Dwarfs

All *Classic Tales* have an accompanying

- **e-Book with Audio Pack** containing the book and the e-book with audio, for use on a computer or CD player. Teachers can also project the e-book onto an interactive whiteboard to use it like a Big Book.
- **Activity Book and Play** providing extra language practice and the story adapted as a play for performance in class or on stage.

For more details, visit www.oup.com/elt/readers/classictales

OXFORD
UNIVERSITY PRESS

Great Clarendon Street, Oxford, OX2 6DP, United Kingdom

Oxford University Press is a department of the University of Oxford. It furthers the University's objective of excellence in research, scholarship, and education by publishing worldwide. Oxford is a registered trade mark of Oxford University Press in the UK and in certain other countries

First published in Classic Tales 2006

2015 2014 2013 2012 2011

10 9 8 7 6 5 4 3 2 1

ISBN: 978 0 19 423946 2

This *Classic Tale* title is available as an e-Book with Audio Pack
ISBN: 978 0 19 423949 3

Also available: *The Goose Girl Activity Book and Play*
ISBN: 978 0 19 423947 9

Printed in China

This book is printed on paper from certified and well-managed sources.

ACKNOWLEDGEMENTS

Illustrated by: Elena Selivanova/Beehive Illustration